Contents

Chapter 1

Practice time

Pedro told his dog, Peppy,

"Tomorrow is the pet show.

I want you to be the best pet!

Let's practise your tricks."

Pedro told Peppy, "Sit!"

Peppy sat.

Pedro said, "Stay."

Peppy stayed.

"Fetch!" said Pedro.

Peppy fetched.

"Good dog!" Pedro smiled.

He gave Peppy a treat.

Then Pedro gave Peppy a

bath.

Peppy did not like baths.

He liked mud much more!

Chapter 2
Show day

The next day was the

pet show.

Pedro saw Katie and her

kitten, Peaches. Peppy liked

Peaches, and Peaches liked

Peppy.

Roddy told Pedro, "My parrot,

Rocky, will win. He is the best."

"Best! Best! BEST!" said Rocky.

Pedro waited for the judge

to come and see Peppy. Pedro

told Peppy, "Sit."

Peppy sat.

He sat on a bee.

TWO bees!

Peppy howled! Peppy

jumped! Peppy ran!

He ran into a muddy puddle.

SPLAT!

Peppy began to shake. He

shook mud all over Pedro.

"You two are a mess!" yelled

Roddy. "No rosettes for you."

Pedro felt sad.

Pedro tried to cheer up.

He watched Pablo's hamster

spinning on his wheel.

"Great spinning!" said the

judge.

Pablo won a rosette.

Pedro saw JoJo and her
bunny, Betty.

Betty won a rosette too. She
won for being soft and furry
and friendly.

Then Pedro saw Katie. She said, "Peaches is shaking. She has never been to a pet show. The noise and smells are scaring her."

The judges saw Roddy's parrot.

"He's the best," bragged Roddy.

Rocky screamed, "Best! Best!

BEST!"

That made

Peaches jump.

Peaches ran away!

Katie chased Peaches, but

Peaches was fast. She ran under

a fence and into the woods!

Chapter 3
Blue-rosette winner

Peppy ran too! He ran after Peaches.

Pedro yelled, "Peppy, FETCH!"

Peppy jumped over the fence.

Peaches was hiding. Peppy

sniffed and sniffed. He found

Peaches!

He picked her up and

jumped back over the fence.

SPLAT!

Peppy landed in the mud.

But he held on to Peaches.

She was safe!

Katie hugged Peaches and

Peppy. She didn't mind getting

muddy.

Pedro patted Peppy over and

over. "Good dog! Good dog!"

The judge told Pedro, "You told Peppy to fetch, and he did! Peppy is the best. He wins the blue rosette!"

"Yay!" Everyone cheered.

When Pedro and
Peppy got home, they
needed a bath.

Guess who liked the
bath the most?

About the author

Fran Manushkin is the author of Katie Woo, the highly acclaimed early-reader series, as well as the popular Pedro series. There is a real Katie Woo: Fran's great-niece, but she doesn't get into as much trouble as the Katie in the books. Fran lives in New York City, three blocks from Central Park, where she can often be found bird-watching and daydreaming. She writes at her dining room table, without the help of her naughty cats, Goldy and Chaim.

About the illustrator

Tammie Lyon began her love for drawing at a young age while sitting at the kitchen table with her dad. She attended the Columbus College of Art and Design, where she earned a bachelor's degree in fine art. After a brief career as a professional ballet dancer, she decided to devote herself full time to illustration. Today she lives with her husband, Lee, in Cincinnati, Ohio, USA. Her dogs, Gus and Dudley, keep her company as she works in her studio.

Glossary

brag to talk in a boastful way about how good you are at something

fetch to go after and bring back something or somebody

howl to cry out in pain or frustration

rosette an award that is made out of colourful fabric

sniff to smell for something

Let's talk

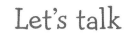

1. How does Pedro feel after Peppy runs into the muddy puddle? What clues tell you how he's feeling?

2. Do you agree that Peppy is the best pet? Why or why not?

3. Think of a pet you know, your own or someone else's. What would that pet win a rosette for?

Let's write

1. How did Pedro prepare Peppy for the pet show? List the steps.

2. List the pets in the story. Which would you like as a pet and why?

3. Make a blue rosette for Peppy. On the rosette, list reasons why Peppy is the winner.

JOKE AROUND

What is a dog's favourite dessert?
Pupcakes!

Knock, knock.
Who's there?
Ken
Ken who?
Ken you walk the dog for me?

What do you call a pile of kittens?
A meowntain

Why are cats great singers?
They are very mewsical.

What was the bunny's favourite game?
Hopscotch

What was the parrot's favourite game?
Hide and speak

HAVE MORE FUN WITH PEDRO!